I0519979

WARNING

This book contains sexually explicit scenes and adult language. It may be considered offensive to some readers. This book is for sale to adults ONLY.

* * * * * * * * * * * * * * * * * * *

Please store your files wisely where they cannot be accessed by underage readers.

Please feel free to send me an email. Just know that these emails are filtered by my publisher. Good news is always welcome.

Just Plain Bob - **justplainbob@awesomeauthors.org**

About the Publisher

4Fun Publishing, a member of **BLVNP Incorporated**, 340 S. Lemon #6200, Walnut CA 91789, info@blvnp.com / legal@blvnp.com
NOTE: Due to the highly emotional reaction of some people to works of erotic fiction, any email sent to the above address that contains foul language or religious references is automatically deleted by our anti-spam software and will not be seen. All other communications are welcome.

DISCLAIMER

Please don't be stupid and kill yourself. This book is a work of FICTION. Do not try any new sexual practice that you find in this book. It is fiction and not to be confused with reality. Neither the author nor the publisher or its associates assume any responsibility for any loss, injury, death or legal consequences resulting from acting on the contents in this book. Every character in this book is over 18 years of age. The author's opinions are not to be construed as the opinions of the publisher. The material in this book is for entertainment purposes ONLY. Enjoy.

Becoming A Shared Wife, Vol. 5
HOT EROTICA

Rachel

A SHARED WIFE SPECIAL

JUST PLAIN BOB

Becoming A Shared Wife, Vol. 5

Rachel

A Shared Wife Special

Hot Erotica

By: Just Plain Bob

© **Just Plain Bob 2014**
ISBN: 978-1-68030-078-9

It was intense! It was by far the strongest orgasm I'd had in quite a while and I wasn't even on a bed. I was bent over the back of the couch in my living room and the hard cock was driving into me from behind. My feet weren't even touching the floor and I had my wadded up panties in my mouth and I was biting down hard on them to keep from screaming out and waking the baby.

He gave one last push, muttered "Oh fuck!" and I felt the hot wetness of his discharge. He stood behind me not moving as his cock lost its hardness and when he was limp he stepped back and his cock flopped out of me. I scooted back until my feet were touching the floor and then I stood and turned to face him and asked:

"What was your name again?"

To understand why a nameless man was plundering my pussy, you need to know only that I'm a girl who was raised by a father whose basic philosophy was:

"Don't get mad, get even and after you are even go a little farther and get ahead."

I heard that all my life and I remembered it on the day I found out what my husband Tony had been up to.

~~***~~

The story starts on the day that Tony said, "I think we are ready for children now. What do you think?"

I stared down at my coffee as I thought about the question. Tony and I had been married just short of five years. We decided even before taking our vows that while we did want children, we did not want them until we had done some traveling, we had done a few things that we wanted to do and we're financially stable. Apparently, Tony thought we were at that point. I wasn't all that happy with my job as a legal secretary and becoming a stay at home mom had a certain appeal for me and so I said:

"I guess that it is as good a time as any."

I took myself off the pill, put my diaphragm in storage and four months later I was, as my mother so quaintly put it, with child and that is when the problems started. Actually, the problems started when I started showing. At the first sign of my enlarging tummy, my sex life started going to hell. Our four and sometimes five times a week fell to three and sometimes four and then to two and on a rare occasion three and that was followed by maybe once a week.

My hormones were raging and I wanted to make love two and three times a day and I wasn't getting it. Finally, Tony stopped making love to me altogether. He told me that he was afraid that making love would hurt the baby. I pointed out that the doctor said we could keep going until the eighth month or until it got uncomfortable for me, but Tony said that doctors have been known to be wrong and he wasn't going to take any chances.

And then, as if the lack of sex wasn't bad enough, Tony came home and told me he was in line for a promotion at work and he was going to have to start putting in longer hours. Just when I was feeling my worst I was being left home alone almost every night of the week. I had my job to keep me occupied during the day, but sitting home alone watching the pap that had on TV just wasn't getting it. I put up with it for about a month and then I started looking for something to do that would get me out of the house in the evenings.

I was at the public library one Monday checking out some books on child rearing when I saw a notice on the bulletin board about a Tuesday night book discussion group. Tuesday night I showed up, had an interesting time, met some nice people and decided to continue attending. The next Tuesday I ended up sitting next to a woman about my age and in talking I found that we had a lot in common. After the meeting, the two of us went to the Waffle House for coffee and to get to know each other better. I found out that Julie's reason for starting to attend the discussion group was the same as mine. She started attending because she also was tired of being home alone while her husband worked late hours.

"Of course it didn't take me long to figure out that what Frank was really doing was boffing his secretary."

"Oh my God! What did you do, leave him?"

"Hell no. I decided that what was good for the gander was good for the goose so I took a lover."

"Did your husband find out?"

"He hasn't yet."

"I don't know how you can do it. If I caught my husband cheating I'd be gone so fast that it would take my shadow a week to catch up to me."

"It is easy to say that and it was what I almost did, but I thought about what it would be like living as a single mom and I decided 'no way.' Why should I give up my comfortable life just because the dipshit was banging the blond bitch that worked for him? Better that I let him support me while I go out and do what he was doing."

"I suppose that is a reasonable way to look at it. I don't know that I could do that though."

"Sure you could honey. You are a sexy looking lady and the guys would flock to you."

"That's sweet of you to say, but I am starting to look like a cow."

"Doesn't matter girl. There are a lot of guys who think that pregnant women are the sexiest thing going. Oh damn, look at the time.

I have to meet my boyfriend over at the saddleback. See you next week?"

"Yes, I'll be there."

Driving home, I thought about Julie and her situation. No way could I stay with a man who cheated on me. I wondered how she could do it.

~~***~~

The next Tuesday, I was running late but when I got to the library, I found that Julie had saved me the seat next to her. After the meeting, we again hit the Waffle House for coffee and conversation.

"I won't have to rush off tonight," Julie said as we sat down in a booth. "My current boyfriend is out of town for two days. Although this would probably be a good time to start looking for his replacement."

"His replacement?"

"It doesn't pay to keep one for too long a time. They start to get possessive and the last thing I want or need are emotional entanglements. I usually keep one for about six weeks and then I find me another one."

"You just pick one, use him and then dump him? Don't they get mad or upset?"

"Nah! Most of them don't want long term relationships any more than I do."

"Sometimes I think that I should find a lover."

"Hubby been bad?"

"In a way, I guess you could say that."

"In what way?"

"He hasn't made love to me since I started showing. I'm climbing walls, but he says he's afraid that he'll hurt the baby."

"Oh, you poor kid. I know just how you feel. My hormones kicked in and turned me into a nymphomaniac when I was pregnant with Kevin. Fortunately for me, asshole wasn't doing his blond, big titted bimbo at the time and he was able to keep me from going too crazy. Have you tried a vibrator?"

"I don't have one."

"There is an adult book store just up the street. Stop and get one on your way home."

"I'd be too embarrassed to go into a place like that."

"Balderdash and poppy-cock! It would do you a world of good to go in there. It would be great for your ego."

"How would be going into an adult book store be great for my ego?"

"There will probably be half a dozen guys in there and every one of them will want to take you into the back where the booths are. One or two may even straight out ask."

"Oh God, now I know I can't go in there."

"I'll go with you."

"Why would you do that?"

"To protect you and keep you from doing something foolish."

"What do you mean by doing something foolish?"

"If you are as horny as I think you are, you just might get weak minded and let yourself be led into the back."

~~***~~

"The key," Julie said as we stood in front of the display of vibrators, dildos and strap-ons, "Is to get something as close in size to hubby's as you can. Get one bigger and you will end up constantly comparing him to the toy and wishing he was larger. Believe me when I say you don't want to go there."

I was looking nervously around the store as Julie was talking. There were seven guys in the store, not counting the guy behind the counter, and they were all looking at Julie and me the way I imagined hungry wolves would look at a baby lamb. A couple of them were fairly hunky looking and I actually did wonder what it would be like to let them take me back to the arcade area. Suddenly:

"Earth to Rachel, come in please," brought me back to the task at hand.

Julie was smiling at me and she said, "Yep! Damned good thing I came along with you."

I'm sure that I must have blushed because she laughed and then said, "Go ahead and pick one." I looked back over to the hunky looking guys and she laughed again. "Vibrators silly, pick a vibrator."

I settled on a pink one close to Tony's size and went up to the counter and paid for it and the man behind the counter took my money, smiled at me and nodded his head slightly toward the entrance of the arcade. I knew what he was asking and I blushed again and hurried away from the counter.

In the parking lot Julie asked me if I was able to get away at any time during the day and I told her that the only time would be my lunch hour from work and then she asked me if I had to rush home from work and I told her that I didn't have to on Monday, Tony's bowling night, or Wednesday which was the night Tony went to his Fraternal Order of Eagles meetings. We made a date for lunch on Thursday and then I headed home. I stopped at a 7-11 and bought batteries for my new pink toy and was looking forward to using it as soon as I reached the house. I thought maybe Tony seeing me use it might make him want some, but I was disappointed in that. When I got home he asked me what I had in the bag and I showed him. He said:

"Good. Now I don't have to feel so guilty."

~~***~~

My lunch date with Julie turned into a weekly thing with us getting together once or twice a week. Julie had a warm and bubbly personality and she had a way of making me laugh even when I was down in the dumps. I started meeting her after work for coffee and occasionally we would stop at a bar or lounge for drinks. Because of my pregnancy I stuck to ginger ale while Julie drank margaritas. If the place had some music - live band or jukebox - and a dance floor, it was inevitable that the two of us were asked to dance. At first I was hesitant, but Julie said:

"You need this honey. Because of your idiot husband you are feeling unwanted and unloved. Most of the guys asking you to dance are doing it because to them you look sexy as all get out."

"No, I don't. I'm getting fat."

"I told you once before that there are plenty of men who think that pregnant women are the sexiest thing going. I guarantee that you could get laid in the next ten minutes if you wanted to."

That was the problem - I did want to. The pink toy had helped a little, but it still left me almost as horny as I was before I used it. It didn't help any that Julie kept up a running commentary on the guys who were there. "Oh look," she said as she pointed out a guy, "Doesn't he have a nice tight looking ass?" She pointed at one guy and said, "Damn, he sure is ugly, but he has big feet and big hands and they do say that big hands and big feet are a sign that he has a big cock. Wouldn't you like a big cock right about now?" And "Don't look now, but that blond over at the jukebox is eyeing you and if that bulge in his jeans is any indication he likes what he sees."

I did break out of my shell a little and I did dance with some of the guys who asked me, but it was a mixed blessing. It was very nice to be held - to have a man's hands touching me - but the stiff cocks being poked into my leg only made me hornier than I already was. I received several invitations to go out to the parking lot and play; to go to a motel and play or to go to his apartment and play, but even as I wished like hell that I could I always remembered my vows to be only Tony's for better or worse. Damn him anyway! The doctor said there would be no problem, but Tony still had the irrational fear that making love to me would somehow hurt the baby.

~~***~~

It was a Tuesday evening and as the discussion group was breaking up, Julie asked me if I would go to the Saddleback lounge with her and keep her company until her current boyfriend met her there. Tony was working late again and we usually stopped for pie and coffee at the Waffle House anyway so I said yes.

I was nursing my ginger ale and Julie was on her second margarita and commenting on the men in the place when I heard her say:

"Oh shit!"

"Oh shit what?"

"One of my ex-boyfriends just came in."

"So why the 'Oh shit.' I thought all of your affairs were short term and you parted friends?"

"Almost all of them were, but he is one of the rare ones I dropped because he made me nervous."

"Nervous how?"

"I don't know. Something about him just didn't seem right. He was lying to me about something - I don't know what - but I sensed it and I don't like being lied to. I'm upfront with the guys I play with. They know I'm married and they know why I play. I expect the same honesty from them. He was good in the sack, but he just made me nervous."

"That doesn't answer the question; why the 'Oh shit?' If he's gone, he's gone."

"When I broke up with him he didn't take it well. He called me a whore, a slut and some other names. I just hope he doesn't see me and come over and make a scene."

I looked over my shoulder and asked, "Which one is he?"

"Over by the door to the kitchen. The guy sitting with the redhead."

I took a look at her ex and said, "He won't come over and make a scene; at least not if he plans on hooking up with the redhead."

"They are probably already hooked up. They came in together."

"How long was he your lover?"

"Just short of a month."

"Recently?"

"He was the one just before the one I'm seeing now."

"So you broke up with him within the last couple of weeks?"

"Three weeks ago."

"Let me make a wild guess here. You saw him mostly on Mondays and Wednesdays."

"How did you know that?"

"Monday is supposed to be his bowling night and Wednesdays is the night he supposedly attends the meetings of the Fraternal Order of Eagles."

Julie's face went pale as what I had just said registered on her. "Oh my God, you don't mean…"

"Fraid I do. That asshole sitting with the redhead is my loving husband. Funny, she doesn't look like work to me."

Julie gave me a confused look and I said, "He is supposed to be working late tonight."

Julie started to say something, but just then a guy walked up to the booth and said, "Sorry I'm late sweetie. I had a flat tire."

Julie introduced me to Chuck and after he sat down I said, "I need to leave you two love birds alone, but how do I get out of here without asshole seeing me?"

"You aren't going to go over there and confront him?"

"Oh no. I'm not sure yet what I'm going to do, but confronting him isn't on the list. At least not right now."

"There is an exit at the end of the hall that leads to the bathrooms," Chuck said, "If you get up and keep your back to him and walk toward the restrooms you should be okay."

I stood up, looked at Julie and asked, "We still on for lunch tomorrow?"

"Are you sure?"

"You didn't know so no harm, no foul. See you tomorrow."

~~***~~

As I drove home the anger I was feeling was causing me to grip the steering wheel so hard my hands hurt. I thought about what I had just discovered about my loving husband and I wondered just how long it had been going on. Was it before I got pregnant or did it start when he couldn't do me because of the baby? Or was the baby the excuse he used because he just didn't want me? But most of all I thought about how I had been home climbing walls because of a lack of sex while that miserable bastard was out fucking whatever he could get his hands on.

The big question was "What was I going to do?" Ideas from murder to just plain castration flowed through me head. In my mind I had a vision of Tony waking up in the morning tied to the bed and seeing me standing there with the knife I used for boning chicken while I reached for his dick, but by the time I pulled into the driveway at the house I knew a couple of things. I knew that Julie was right in that life as a single mom would suck and that giving up a comfortable life would be senseless. I didn't know if I could take on lovers like Julie, but even if I did what could Tony say about it if he found out?

By the time I set my purse down on the table I had decided that I was going to do nothing for the time being. I would behave as if I had no clue as to what Tony was doing. It wouldn't be all that difficult. I wouldn't flinch when he touched me in bed since he hadn't done that in weeks and if he noticed any change in me when I was around him I would blame it on hormonal changes brought on by the pregnancy. I made sure that I was in bed pretending to be asleep when the asshole got home.

~~***~~

Julie was already sitting at a table when I entered Spiro's and I could see a touch of concern on her face. I sat down across from her and asked:

"You finding this difficult?"

"I don't know how to behave. I've never had lunch with the wife of one of lovers at least not knowingly."

"Like I told you last night, you didn't know so I'm not holding it against you, but even so it is what I want to talk about today. I want to know everything. What, when, where and how. Not the details of what you did in the sack obviously, but where you met him and things like that."

"Why would you want to know all that?"

"Because one of these days we will have it out and I'm going to want all the ammunition I can get."

"Well, let's see. It was about five weeks ago and I had just dumped Ivan. It was a Wednesday night and I was having a drink after work at The Front Page with some of the girls I work with. There was a live band and men were coming over to our table and asking us to dance. Tony asked me to dance several times and I knew what he was looking for and by the fourth or fifth dance I decided to take a chance on him. We used the Quality Inn on Westin and 43rd. He knew my story and why I was playing around. It was on our third or fourth date when he started in with a bunch of macho bullshit about making Frank cuckold, about being more of a man than Frank was that I started feeling uneasy with him. That and I sensed that he was lying when he talked about his own marriage."

"Why? Just what did he say?"

Julie looked away and I said, "Come on, give. You won't upset me. You have already admitted that you believed he was lying to you."

"He said you were a cold fish in bed. He said you always wore a flannel night gown and would only pull it up to your waist when you had sex. There was no foreplay because you thought sex for fun was dirty and the only reason for having sex was to produce children. He said you would only have sex with him when you were in your fertile period and that as soon as you got pregnant you cut him off. He said you put him in a position where in order to have any sex life at all, he had to cheat on you."

"Did he tell you why he would marry someone like that?"

"He said he didn't know how you were until after the wedding. He told me you were a virgin who wouldn't give it up until you were married. He expected you to be a firecracker in the sack based on the hot make out sessions you had while you were dating. He said he felt you deliberately led him on to get him to marry you."

"Then why on Earth would he stay in a marriage like that if he felt that way?"

"According to him he was already planning on a divorce, but then you got pregnant and he felt that he had to stay with you and be a father to the child."

"That certainly is mighty big of him."

"Hey! He's an asshole and we both know it. Know what you are going to do yet?"

"No. I'm like you in that life as a single mother living in an apartment somewhere doesn't appeal to me, but it chaps my ass that he is getting laid and I'm climbing walls because I'm not."

"You can always do what I'm doing to get back at Frank."

"That's the problem Julie; I don't think I can do something like that."

"Bullshit honey. If I had not been with you the night you bought that vibrator, you would have been in the back of that arcade doing all the guys who were in the store that night. I saw the way you looked at them."

I thought back to that night and I think that I might have blushed because Julie giggled.

"I wasn't looking at all of them, just one of the hunkier ones."

"Rachel honey, I don't know if you have ever pulled a train before, but believe me when I tell you that if the hunky one would have gotten you in the back, you would have pulled one that night."

"Doesn't matter anyway. I'm starting to look like a beached whale and I couldn't attract a lover."

"Bet me! I can see two guys in here right now who haven't taken their eyes off of you since you walked in. I keep telling you that there are tons of guys who think pregnant women are sexy. I'll bet you anything you would care to bet that if you meet me when you get off work tonight I can have you laid by eight o'clock."

"You really think so?"

"Honey, I don't just think - I know! Come on and give it a shot. You don't need to hurry home. Tonight is his lodge meeting night, right?"

"Yeah, but he normally comes home for dinner before he goes out."

"So for one night he can do leftovers while you pull on him what he pulls on you. You call him and tell him that you are working late tonight."

I thought about it. I didn't really think I could attract anyone being in the condition I was in, but right then I really wasn't in the mood to go home and have to look at the cheating bastard I had married. I was about to say, "Okay, lets do it," when I had a thought.

"How do we know we won't run into Rob? Tonight is one of his cheating nights and he will be out on the prowl. How do we know we won't both end up at the same place?"

"Do you care? Do you really care? He is supposed to be at a meeting exchanging secret passwords and secret handshakes and whatever other nonsense they do. If you run into him you get your confrontation sooner rather than later. But you do stop with your co-workers after work for a drink every now and then and he knows the places you stop, right? I'm betting that he never goes to any of those places because he is afraid he will run into you or someone who knows him and who might tell you. What do you say? We going to do it?"

"I'm not sure Julie. I don't know if I can do it."

"Okay, so you don't do it, but you still need to stop with me so the guys have a chance to take a shot at you and show you that you are a sexy and desirable woman. Come on Rachel, if for no other reason than your ego needs a boost."

I thought Julie was just being nice to me, but I really didn't want to go straight home after work and face my cheating asshole of a husband so I told Julie I would stop with her.

~~***~~

I had a mouthful of pillow and was biting down hard to keep from screaming as the hard cock pushed deep into me from behind. I had already cum twice and a third time was fast approaching. Out of the corner of my eye I saw Julie on the other bed sucking Chuck's cock trying to get him up again and I wondered if I had enough time to do the same thing to my guy. After such a long dry spell, I certainly wanted to keep going, but I did need to beat Tony home. If I was going to do more of what I was doing I needed to keep Tony from even remotely considering that I might be getting what he wouldn't give me someplace else. That meant that I was going to have to maintain the appearance of a happy housewife which in turn meant that Tony had to believe that I was sitting home fat, dumb and happy while he was out catting around.

And I was going to do more of what I was doing. A lot more!

"Ready baby?" my lover asked. "Want me to pull out?"

"Don't you dare," I moaned as he gripped my hips, drove hard and fast into me and I felt the hot liquid heat of his discharge. He pushed into me until he started to soften and then he pulled out. I rolled over onto my back and looked up at him looking down at me.

"You are one hell of a hot lady," he said and I grinned at him and said, "You aren't too bad yourself."

I glanced at my watch and then said, "I've got time for one more if you have a fast recovery time."

"With a little help I don't think it would take too long."

"An invitation if I ever heard one. Bring it to me."

He moved so that his cock was next to my mouth and I started giving him head. As my mouth worked on his dick I thought back to earlier in the evening. Julie and I had no sooner sat down and placed our drink order than two guys moved in on us and asked us to dance. I was not ready for how fast the guy I was dancing with made his move. He said that he had noticed my rings and the quick way I had said yes to his asking me to dance made him think that I might just be on the prowl and then he flat out asked me if I would like to go to a motel with him. I was caught a little flat footed and said:

"It is a little early in the evening for me to be making major decisions. Why don't we wait and see."

"Okay then, may I join you at your table? If I don't stake my claim early I'm going to be just one in a long line of guys trying to get you."

"That was a sweet think to say to an old, fat married lady."

"A very sexy married lady."

His name was Curt and I did let him join me at the table. By then, Julie had already informed Curt's buddy that she didn't mind dancing with him or letting him buy her drinks, but she had a boyfriend who would be coming along latter on. The guy said no problem and he would keep her company until her boyfriend arrived.

By the time Chuck arrived, dancing with Curt had me horny as a goat. It was obvious that he wanted me and that was all it really took although the hard cock that kept poking me did help some. As soon as Chuck had downed one drink and had danced once with Julie she announced to the table that the dancing and drinking were over.

"It is time to get my girlfriend laid."

Ten minutes later, we were in room 213 of the Quality Inn on Westin and 43rd and I thought it only fitting that I was about to have my first extramarital affair at the same motel where Tony had his first time with Julie.

I got Curt hard and he fucked me one more time. When it was over and I was dressing he asked if he could see me again.

"You really want to?"

"Oh yeah!"

"I can only do it on Mondays, Wednesdays and on nights my husband works late."

"That will work for me. I'll give you my cell number so you can call me when he works late."

"Why? Why is a good looking guy like you wanting to waste his time on a fat married woman?"

"Honestly?"

"Of course."

"It is the fact that you are married and pregnant that is the major turn on. I think pregnant women are sexy and there is something just so cool about making it with another man's woman."

"Well, that certainly is romantic."

"You wanted honesty, I gave you honesty. My reading of you is that you aren't looking for romance. You are getting even with hubby for something and I was in the right place at the right time. I think you are one hell of a hot lady and I'll take what I can get for as long as I can get it, but I don't see you in this for the long haul. Am I wrong?"

I smiled at him and shook my head no and then said, "You pretty much summed it up." I exchanged a pretty passionate kiss with him and told him I would see him on Monday. He got in his pick up truck and drove off and as I watched his tail lights disappear I was thinking:

"Okay girl, you are now officially an adulteress which is something that you never ever expected to be."

I had been a bit of a 'wild child' before I met Tony. I'd done a threesome or two and once I even pulled a four man train when I'd gotten high at a party at a frat house, but I thought that when I said "I do" those days were history. I smiled a little as I thought about the four man 'train' and wondered how Tony would take it if his pregnant wife were to pull a train and he were to find out about it.

"Is that the smile of a sexually satisfied woman or are you smiling for some other reason?"

"Both," I said, and then I told Julie what I had just been thinking.

"Oh my. I never would have thought that sweet, young and innocent looking you could have done such things. Maybe I should have you go in the back of the arcade that night."

"I wonder if they are still there."

"Maybe not the same ones, but I'll bet there are some others there. Why? Are you thinking of going back and playing."

"It is a thought. Tonight was as much about sticking it to Tony as it was about getting me laid. I can just imagine his face if I were to smile and tell him "You wouldn't make love to me because you were afraid to hurt the baby, but nothing happened to the baby when I was gangbanged by ten guys." He would just shit!"

"You would do ten?"

"Probably not that many."

"But you would do a gangbang?"

"Yeah, I probably would just so I could throw it in Tony's face."

"I've never even done two guys at once, let alone a gangbang. If I set one up for you could I watch?"

"You've never done one, but you know how to set one up?"

"Don't forget I've been hanging horns on Frank for over two years now. I've stayed on good terms with a lot of my ex-lovers and I'm sure I could get some of them to do it."

"I'll keep it in mind, but I don't think I'm quite ready for something like that just yet.

~~***~~

I met Curt after work on Monday and we spent three hours in his apartment. That was the start of my three week affair with him. It ended on a good note. He met a girl he was interested in and we parted friends. He was followed by Tom who was followed by Jack who was replaced by Travis.

I was just starting my eighth month when Julie asked, "Are you still interested in a gangbang?"

"I haven't thought much about it. Why?"

"I just thought that if you were going to do it while you are pregnant you are almost out of time."

She kept glancing away and suddenly it clicked. "Bullshit! This isn't about me at all. It is about you. You want to see a gangbang and you see me as your best chance."

She shrugged her shoulders and I said, "But you are right about my doing it while I am pregnant. I will want to be able to rub Tony's nose in it when we finally have it out. You said you could set one up. Make it for next Monday."

"How many?"

"Six to eight, but no more than eight."

"Why that number?"

"You'll see. And make sure that the ones you get won't mind being video taped or having their pictures taken."

"Why?"

"Because I want a visual record of the event for down the road."

~~***~~

I was a little nervous as I looked around the room and at the seven men who stood there watching me. I wanted to do it and didn't want to do it at the same time. I didn't want to do it because I was married and in my mind this was something that a married woman shouldn't be doing. On the other hand, I wanted to do it, tape it and show the tape to Tony and say:

"Here. Watch this you cheating bastard!"

I took a deep breath and then said, "There are some rules that need to be followed guys. No rough stuff, no marks on me and no double penetrations except for vaginal and oral."

"How about your ass if it isn't part of a double?" asked a hunky looking redhead.

I didn't like anal sex and I never let Tony have any even though he was always asking for it. But then I had the thought that what this was all about was sticking it to Tony, wasn't it? And I was going to get it on film to show him some day so why not suck it up and let it happen?

"I don't usually do anal, but this is a special occasion. If you use plenty of lube and go real slow and easy I'll allow it."

"What's your preference, Astroglide or KY?" the redhead asked.

"Doesn't matter as long as you use plenty."

"Be right back," he said as he headed for the door.

While he was gone the guys cut cards to set up the rotation. Julie cut for the redhead and then we laid out the sequence. Number one would be first in my pussy while I sucked on number two. When one came, two would take his place in my pussy and number three would move to my mouth and so on until everyone had gone one time and then the redhead (whose name was Asa) would do my ass and then after that we would see.

Julie moved to where she had a good angle and she started videotaping as the action started. While I sucked on Steve (#2), John (#1) slid his cock into me and fucked me to two good orgasms before he came. He moved away and Steve took his place in my pussy while Mark (#3) moved to where I could get my mouth around his cock. After that, I didn't bother to keep track as the men moved in to use me.

I was not surprised when I saw Steve with the video camera in his hands and taping the action. I had known all along that Julie would not be able to just watch. Over on the left, I saw her on her hands and knees as John took her from behind while sucked Mark's cock.

I was surprised that I didn't have more orgasms than I had. I guess that it was because I really wasn't into doing the gangbang. I was only doing it to spite Tony and so that I could shove the tape of the affair up his nose and not because I had any huge sexual hunger that I needed to have satisfied. Don't get me wrong - I enjoyed it - but it just wasn't a hot sexual turn on.

When Jim (#7) was done, Asa (who had been #5) was hard again and ready to try my ass. I concentrated on sucking Jerry's (#4) cock while Asa worked on my butt hole with the KY jelly. He started with one finger and then two and finally three. When he touched the head of his cock to my butt hole, I took my mouth off of Jerry because I knew it was going to hurt and I didn't want to bite Jerry's cock off when the pain hit and I clenched my teeth.

I told Mark who had the camera at the time to stop filming until I got the pain part out of the way. Asa went slow and easy as he worked his cock into me. I kept from screaming and hollering by biting down on the pillow that I had in my mouth. After several minutes, the pain faded to discomfort and I told Mark to start filming again and I made sure that the camera caught me looking as if I loved being butt fucked even though I didn't. By the time Asa was ready to shoot his load in my ass, the discomfort had given way to a pleasurable sensation. However, the pleasure I experienced was not worth the pain it took me to get to that point, but having reached that point it made it easier to take on the next three who wanted to try my ass.

Then I set up the final shot on the tape. The camera caught the cum dripping from my mouth as Hank (#6) pulled his cock out of it and then the camera panned to show the cum dripping from my ass as John pulled out. After that, the camera was set aside and for the next two hours, the seven took turns fucking Julie and me. The high point for me was watching Asa, Hank and Jerry making Julie "air tight."

As we showered I said, "Now you know why I wanted so many."

"You knew I'd get pulled into it?"

"I would have bet money on it."

"It was wild. I think I'd like to do it again."

"Well honey, you already have the list of guys willing to do it."

"When do you want to do it again?"

"I don't. This was a one time thing for me so I can rub Tony's nose in it when the time comes. I'll be there for moral support if you want me there, but I'm not interested in doing it again. Besides, in three weeks I'm going to have the baby and then I'll be out of commission for at least six weeks."

"What happens then? Will you still be with the asshole?"

"I don't know. But I do know one thing. If we are still together on the day the doctor clears me to have sex again the first person to do me will not be Tony. He may not even get to be second or third."

"I don't know girl, but to me that sounds like gangbang."

"Maybe a mini one. We will just have to wait and see."

~~***~~

I was on my knees in front of Travis licking his cock when my water broke. Travis rushed me to the hospital and when I got there, I called Tony on his cell. He wanted to know how I got to the hospital and I told him I took a cab. Before Travis left, I apologized for not finishing him and promised him he would be my first when I was cleared to have sex again. The last thing I did before things got really busy for me was call Julie and let her know where I was. She couldn't visit because I never wanted Tony to see the two of us together, but at least she would know why she couldn't get in touch.

During the pregnancy, we had all the tests and checks done, but we told everyone that we didn't want to know the sex of the child - we wanted it to be a surprise. Tony kept betting me that it was a boy because of how big I got and I kept letting him believe that. Lisa Anne came into the world at eight pounds even and I felt that the Gods were smiling on me because Tony had his heart set on a son. But even so, he couldn't wait to start handing out cigars. He kept telling me that we built beautiful babies and that the next time we would have a boy.

I was home after a two-day stay at the hospital and since Tony was at work, Julie was able to stop by the house for coffee on her way to work or on her way home. We talked about everything under the sun, but the one thing that Julie kept coming back to was the gang bang. I told her to go ahead and set it up and I'd be there to offer moral support and that is why I found myself in a hotel room with her three weeks after Lisa was born.

She had five guys there and things were moving along nicely as Julie was being triple penetrated while the other two stroked their cocks and waited their turn. I was sitting in the easy chair holding Lisa Anne when she started to fuss and fret. I didn't even think about it as I opened up my clothing and offered her a fat, milk filled breast to suck on. She latched onto the nipple and went to work and I stopped paying attention to what Julie and her playmates were doing. That is I stopped paying attention until I felt hot breath on my neck and opened my eyes to see that one of the two waiting guys with his face almost down to where Lisa's was. His name was Hank and I knew him vaguely since he had been at my gang bang and I was surprised when he asked:

"Could I have a taste?"

"I don't think Lisa would like it if I pulled her loose right now."

"There's the other one. I'd just like a taste."

He was serious and the more I thought about it the more I thought, why not? One more thing I could tell Tony about when the time came. I popped the other breast out and Hank went to work on it. With two mouths on me it was inevitable that I was going to get horny and I did. I closed my eyes and leaned my head back against the chair and thought of fucking Travis in another couple of weeks. I was moaning and I felt something touch my lips and I opened my eyes and saw the other waiting guy, Tom something, with his cock against my lips. I moaned and his cock slid into my mouth.

What a sight it must have been. One man sucking on my right tit, my baby nursing on the left and a cock sawing in and out of my mouth. Tom came and I swallowed what he pushed out and after him it was Hank and then a couple of the other guys. I sucked six cocks while I sat there and held Lisa and swallowed what they produced as the guys used me as a "fluffer" to get them back up so they could get back to Julie. It made me feel guilty because I had promised Travis he could be first when I got back to doing it. Julie said she was stunned when she looked over and saw what I was doing.

"You can't kid me Rachel. You might have said no more gangbangs but if the doctor had cleared you for sex before you got here today you would have put Lisa in her tote, stuck a bottle in her mouth and you would have been right in there with me."

At that exact instant I couldn't have denied it.

~~***~~

From the day of Lisa's arrival, Tony was a changed man. He hovered over Lisa and me and spoiled us rotten. It was "what can I get you baby" and "what do you need honey" and "what can I do to make things easier." Monday night arrived and he didn't leave for bowling and when I asked him what was going on he said he had arranged for a substitute to fill in for him so he could be around until I got back on my feet. The same thing happened on Wednesday.

"I'm not one of the officers so I can miss a few meetings and it won't hurt."

The fifth week he went back to bowling and his meeting. Of course, he didn't have a clue that I knew bowling and the Eagles were bogus. Well, the Eagles weren't totally bogus. He was a member and we had attended several of their Saturday night dances, but he never went to meetings.

My six week check up was coming up and Tony was getting antsy. I finally had to tell him that it wasn't automatic that I would be given the go ahead at the check up.

"Some women have had to wait as long as three months before the doctor let them go back to playing."

I was fairly certain that I would be given the green light so I called Travis and told him to keep Wednesday afternoon clear. Wednesday came and Dr. Wilkins told me I was good to go so when I left his office I went straight to see Travis. On the way I called Tony on his cell.

"Didn't want you to get your hopes up before you came home. I'm sorry baby, but the doctor says it will be at least one more week. I'll tell you about it when you get home."

I put Lisa in her tote and gave her a bottle and then I stripped.

"You have to go slow and easy with me lover," I told Travis, "I need to get used to it again."

Travis did me twice and I finished the blowjob I owed him and then I gathered up Lisa and headed for home. On the way, I called Julie and gave her the good news.

"I've decided to do a mini gangbang. Can you get me three guys for Monday?"

"Any particular ones?"

"No, just any three of the guys we used before, but if one of them is Asa make sure that you tell him that my butt is off limits."

"Will do."

"Coffee tomorrow?"

"Denny's at ten?"

"That will work."

I was fixing dinner when Tony got home and the disappointment on his face would have made me smile if I wasn't trying so hard to pretend to be just as disappointed as he was. Knowing that all most men knew about a vagina is that it was where you inserted a dick and that some women got happy if you licked it, I spun Tony a tale about distended vaginal walls and swollen membranes and that the doctor thought it would be another week before he would okay intercourse.

"Don't forget baby, I'm only five one and that was an eight pound bundle that came out of that little hole down there. I'm just as disappointed as you are sweetie. It has been a long time for me and mentally, I am more than ready."

Then all of a sudden it was get me off my feet and make sure I got plenty of rest. He did the dishes and cleaned the kitchen. He did a load of laundry and gave Lisa her bath and changed her. When he left for work the next morning, he told me not to do anything except care for Lisa and leave everything else for him. I was shaking my head in disbelief when he left the house. It was just so unreal!

I decided to do just what he said and leave everything for him which gave me enough free time to go over to Travis's apartment for three hours in the middle of the afternoon. It was sure nice having a boyfriend who worked out of his house. It made things so much easier. I wasn't surprised when Tony called me and said he would be working late. He did tell me again not to do anything except take care of Lisa and make a list for him if I had things that needed to be done.

I spent Saturday and Sunday being pampered by Tony and at eleven on Monday morning, I entered the motel room that Julie had gotten and found seven guys there. I looked at Julie and she giggled and said:

"The others are mine."

I looked at the seven and tried to decide which three to choose then decided to hell with it. I ended up doing all of them once and Steve and Mark twice. The most surprising thing about it was that Lisa, who almost never went more than a hour without fussing, was quiet the entire time I was in that motel room.

Tony skipped bowling and stayed home with me that night and again he did everything while I rested on the couch. Tuesday, I went over to visit Travis for two hours and Tuesday evening I left Lisa with Tony and I went to the book discussion group. Over coffee at the Waffle House, I asked Julie if she could get me three guys for eleven o'clock the next morning and she said she could handle it.

"Just three kiddo! None of that 'extra for you' stuff. I have something special in mind and three guys twice each is all I want."

"I can watch, can't I?"

"You will be watching through the viewfinder sweetie."

I arrived at room 222 and found that Julie had lined me up with Mark, Jeff and Mike. After setting Lisa up with a bottle I had Jeff, who had the skinniest cock, work on my asshole with a lot of KY and then I let him fuck me there to open me up while I sucked off Mike. Once Jeff had cum in my ass, I had all three of the guys move off to the side so the camera wouldn't pick them up and I arranged my naked self on the bed and got out my cell phone. I pointed at Julie and she started taping. I put the cell on 'speakerphone' and called Tony.

"Hello?"

"Good news sweetie. The doctor says I'm good to go. You want dinner or dessert first when you get home tonight?"

"Dessert baby, most definitely dessert."

"Any chance you might be able to get home a little early? I don't want to sound eager, but it has been a while for me."

"Sorry honey, but no way can I get out of here early today, but I will break the speed limit coming home."

"I'll be waiting."

I disconnected and tossed the phone aside and then said, "Okay guys, who gets to be first?"

For three hours it was solid suck and fuck. I did my first ever triple penetration and I let all three guys have my ass. When it was over, I showered and as I toweled dry I watched Julie as she picked up where I left off. She was being three holed as I was heading for the door and I told I'd call her the next day and I think she said "okay" but it is hard to understand what someone is saying when they have a cock in their mouth.

~~***~~

His "Baby, I'm home" was met by "I'm in the bedroom honey." When he walked in he was greeted by the flickering light of a dozen candles and the sight of me lying on the bed in a black lace night gown and 'come fuck me' pumps. He stripped and climbed into bed and I moaned:

"Get it wet baby, get it ready."

He lowered his head and licked the pussy that had been well used by three other cocks only hours before. I just wished I had been brave enough to have left some of their juices in me. He licked and lapped for a couple of minutes and then I moaned:

"Enough lover, I want you in me now. Hurry baby, it's been so long."

As he moved up on me I said, "Be careful and go slow honey, I'm still just a little sore and I'm still a little loose. It takes a while for that little hole to close up after a bundle the size of Lisa comes out of it."

Tony made slow and easy love to me and when he came he fell to the bed next to me and asked:

"Think we could go a second time?"

"Let's not rush things honey. It may take us a while to work back up to more than once every two or three days."

~~***~~

That was a year ago. It took Tony almost six months to get up to three times a week and usually only once on those times. My lovers do a lot better than that. They might only average three times a week, but they usually average three times when we do get together.

Travis met a girl and we kissed goodbye. He was replaced by Jeff who was replaced by Dale and Dale has been my squeeze for the last four months. It turns out that Tony does bowl on Mondays - at least sometimes. He isn't on a team, but he is on a list of substitutes. I've not done any more gangbangs, I do do a few DPs when Julie and I and our dates end up in the same motel room on nights that Tony has to "work late" or following our book discussion group on Tuesday.

I have adopted Julie's philosophy. Better to hang in there and let the asshole support you than go off and be in a small apartment trying to make it as a single mom. I give Tony a good home and I give him an adequate sex life. He has good meals, clean clothes, clean house and with the exception of the sex life, he could have had his life is no different than that of his many married friends.

We go out and party, we play cards with friends and our married life is indistinguishable from a million others except that he is a cheating husband and I am a wife who spends a good deal of her time getting even. I will sit on the tapes for I don't know how long - maybe forever. I know that I won't show them to him unless we break up and it won't matter whether it is his fault or mine.

There is one other piece of revenge that I've taken. On Lisa's first birthday, Tony asked if it was maybe time for us to try for a boy and I laughed at him:

"No way honey. No more kids for me. I like my sex too much. I'm not about to forget the seven months I went without when I was pregnant with Lisa. It got so bad there for a while that the mailman almost got lucky. I'm not going through that again."

He wants a son and he keeps after me and I know that I could still be well fucked during a pregnancy even if not by Tony, but I won't ever give in on that one. That is my ultimate revenge on him. Julie tells me that I'm wrong. She says the ultimate would be to have some other guy's baby. Just pick some guy who looks a lot like Tony. It's a thought, but I don't think I'm ready for something like that.

~~***~~

Which brings me to the nameless guy pounding my pussy. Tony had left for work and Julie had called me and told me that Frank was out of town and that she had hooked up with two guys the night before and they had kept at her all night.

"Sam had to go home, but Tommy still wants to fuck and I have to go to work. I hate to see a hard on as nice as his go to waste. You doing anything right now?"

"What you are telling me is that he is very good, right?"

"Exceptional."

"Send him over."

He arrived at eight-ten and I answered his ring as naked as the day I was born. I led him into the living room, bent over the back of the couch and then turned and smiled at him and when he was done I asked him what his name was.

"Tom."

"Well Tom, let's take this to the bedroom and find out how much staying power you have."

On the way, I made a mental note to call Julie and give her a "thank you."

The End

Here is a sample from another story you may enjoy:

JUST PLAIN BOB

WIVES
Who Stray
BECOMING A SHARED WIFE, VOL. 3

EROTICA COLLECTION

All I was doing was giving my wife a gift. Giving her something that she would truly enjoy and remember for the rest of her life. But what I did was cause her to become a slut and in the process I most probably destroyed our twenty-five year marriage.

Connie and I married right out of college and she has kept me the happiest man in the world for almost twenty-five years. She has been loving, caring, supportive, a fantastic lover and my best friend and I wanted to do something for her to show her just how much I loved and appreciated her. The gift I gave her was no ordinary gift. I loved her enough to swallow my pride, bury my ego and give her something that I knew she had always wanted and something that I personally could not deliver. I gave her another man. More specifically, I gave her a man with a large penis.

Connie and I had a marvelous sex life. Granted, it did slacken after the first full bloom of marriage, going from nightly (sometimes two or three times) to six nights, then five and eventually to four, but we still made love at least four times a week and usually more than once. Other times, we might go all week without making love once and then go seven or eight times over the weekend. Whatever, we still wanted each other and never got in a rut.

One of the things that kept our sex life interesting was pornography. Early in our marriage, we went to a party one night and downstairs in the recreation room they had a porn video playing on the TV. Neither Connie nor I had ever seen anything like that before and it turned us in. When we got home, we spent the rest of that night and most of the next day doing what we saw on that tape. We tried every position that we could and tried to duplicate everything we had seen. That night was the first time for either of us trying anal sex and Connie found that she enjoyed it and it became a regular part of our lovemaking. From that night on, we would rent a porno tape at least once a week and then try out every move and position we saw. I know that to most people the tapes all look the same, but Connie and I always seemed to find something new in each of them.

The one thing those tapes all had in common was that the actors all had such large dicks. In fact, it is probably a given that if you are a man and you want to work in the porno industry, you have to have a bigger than average dick. Playing sports in high school and serving in the Army meant a lot of time spent in shower rooms with other guys and so I know that I'm pretty average as far as penis size goes. I saw some larger, and quite a few smaller, but most guys seemed to have about what I had – six or so inches. Even though I have always satisfied Connie, hardly ever failing to bring her to orgasm, she was still aware of the fact that there were bigger dicks out there in the world.

We would be watching a movie and all of a sudden she would say something like, "My God, look at the size of that thing. How in God's name can she take all that?" Once when I asked her what she wanted for Christmas she laughed and said, "Peter North would be nice." I got her a Jeff Stryker dildo instead. Some time later, I found an ad in a man's magazine for poster sized porno stars and I ordered all sixteen of the male posters and gave Connie one on every Christmas and birthday until I ran out. She always got a kick out of them and said:

"You know that someday you are going to have to get me the real thing."

If you enjoyed this sample then look for **Wives Who Stray.**

Here is another preview of a story you may also enjoy:

The Red

PEONY

EROTIC ROMANCE

Denise Denton

The narrow village road looked the same. Nothing had changed since she left a few years ago. Time had left her home village behind. There were no new houses and the old ones were just as she remembered them, each set back away from the road and surrounded by flowering bushes and fruit trees.

No one was out and about at this time of day. Most of the villagers would be tending their vegetable plots and rice fields. Anna walked to a small wooden house raised five feet above the ground on short, stout timber beams.

She took off her shoes and using the dipper, scooped water from the big urn next to the steps and washed her feet, the way all the villagers did before entering their homes.

She climbed up the six steps, crossed the small verandah to the closed door. It was not locked. None of the villagers had cause to lock their homes. Everyone knew everybody and strangers never pass their way. It was as if their village had been forgotten and it remained as it had always been. Simple wooden houses were built raised off the ground in case the heavy monsoon rains caused the small stream running by the village to overflow and flood the surroundings. There were no fences, only well-worn paths leading off to the twenty or so homes, each well-tended and boasting a variety of flowering shrubs, potted plants and fruit trees.

Anna walked into the small living room. All was quiet except for the cat that purred, opening her eyes as she sensed Anna.

"Putih!" Anna called out and the cat padded over to her, rubbing its head against Anna's bare ankles.

Anna carried her small suitcase into the back room. It had not changed. The single bed with a dresser next to the window, was neatly made. The wooden chair beside the bed was still there. On it sat the cushion embroidered with a prowling tiger. The tiger stared at her, its eyes probing her innermost secrets. The cushion was one of a set of two. She had bought the set as the tiger embodied a life-changing experience for her and Song. She had given the other cushion to Song as a potent reminder of how close they came to be a meal for the tiger. Song, his name threatened to push her into places she had no wish to revisit.

She had come home. This was the room of her childhood and adolescence, her refuge from the storms that had ripped her life apart at a tender age. Her grandparents had taken her in and raised her in this little village ever since she was five.

She looked at the photographs hanging on the wall. There were three altogether.

One showed Anna as a young child with her parents, Zul and Ainee.

The second showed Anna in school uniform clutching a trophy, flanked by her beaming grandparents.

The third showed Anna alone, with the iconic Petronas Twin Towers of Kuala Lumpur in the background.

Her life history depicted by these three photographs left big blanks that strained the curiosity of those who had come to know Anna and visited her village home.

The dream did not fade over time, not like her grandma had said it would. She used to wake up screaming, cowering in fear and her grandma would rush in and hold her, rocking her gently, murmuring words of love and assurance until her sobs subsided into hiccups and she fell asleep in Grandma's arms.

As she grew older, she learned to stifle her screams with her pillow and not wake her grandparents because they had to get up early to tend to their rice field about half a kilometer away from their village.

The first photograph triggered sketchy memories of her parents.

Her mother was a beautiful woman with big flashing eyes and red lips that often parted in a wide smile. Her father was short, like her grandfather, but had broad shoulders. Anna remembered his strong arms whenever he lifted her into the air and she would scream in delight. She also remembered the big fights whenever mama came home late and there was no dinner on the table for papa, no dinner for Anna, who had been alone in the flat when papa unlocked the front door.

If you enjoy this sample then look for **The Red Peony by Denise Denton.**

Also by this Author:

The Prodigal Family: The Abbotts

Watching My Shared Wife

The Waitress and the Runaway Husband

Baiting Mr. Little

Too Hot for Henry

Chuck's Fantasy

Wife Sharing and Other Adventures

The Redhead's Desires

Rescued at Riley's

Hazardous Wives

Wives Who Stray

His Every Fantasy

Open Mike Night

Pursuit for Revenge

From the Author

If you enjoyed any of my books then please share the love and promote my books in Amazon.

If you write me a review and send me an email I will send you a free book, or many.
(Just know that these emails are filtered by my publisher.)

Good news is always welcome.

One Last Thing, For Kindle Readers...

When you turn the page, Kindle will give you the opportunity to rate this book and share your thoughts on Facebook and Twitter. If you enjoyed my writings, would you please take a few seconds to let your friends know about it? Because... when they enjoy they will be grateful to you and so will I.

Thank You!

An Open Letter from Just Plain Bob

A message for those who like my stories, those who hate my stories, those who are indifferent and those who have yet to make up their minds.

I have often stated that I really don't care what others think about my stories, that I write for my own enjoyment and then I offer to share. If you like my stories fine and if you don't, also fine since I have already satisfied my target audience - me!

It is human nature to strive to get better. If you take up bowling your first games are going low scoring, but you will work and practice to get better and as your average climbs you may forget the game where you had three gutter balls and shot an eighty-six, but that game is still there in your past.

Your first time on the golf course you shot an eighty on the front nine, but did you settle for that being your game or did you work to improve? You may eventually get a three handicap, but that nine hole eighty is still there as part of your past.

When you hired in at your job did you say, "Cool, I got it made" and do nothing more than what you barely had to do or did you go to work thinking that, "Someday I'm going to be running this place." You might never climb that high, but human nature says that you are going to at least try.

It is the same with authors who write stories and post them on sites like Literotica. Their first stories might not be all that good, but comments and feedback along with a desire to get better drive them toward putting out a better product or to at least try.

I'm no different. My first stories might not have been all that great, but they are still there on the hard drive. I like cheating wife stories and five years ago I found my first adult site that catered to cheating wife stories. It was a pay site, but it had a policy of giving a free lifetime membership to anyone who submitted five stories to the site. How hard can that be I said to myself as I sat down and fired up the word processor and went to work.

I sent my five stories in and sat back to enjoy my free membership and a funny thing happened. I started getting feedback, most of it positive, and I became hooked. I started cranking out more stories. The site I was sending my stories to had seven categories:

Bisexual
Cream Pie

Groups
I Watch
Gang Bang
Racial
SM/BD

I know nothing about bisexual or SM/BD and I had no interest in Groups so all the stories I wrote I tailored for the four remaining categories:

Cream Pie
I Watch
Gang Bang
Racial.

I turned out eight stories a month, two for each category, which means that after five years I have over 120 stories in each of those categories and they are all still on the hard drive.

A year ago I received an email asking me why I never posted stories on Literotica. The answer? I didn't know about Lit. I pulled it up, liked what I saw, and started sending in stories to it. All new stories? No, not hardly, not with over 400 stories sitting on the hard drive. Maybe one new story for each fifteen or so old ones. The newer ones are better, at least I think they are and I have received some feedback that leads me to believe that others think so too, and I will continue to write new ones.

But I am still going to recycle what is on the hard drive, stories that were written specifically to fit the four categories. That means that those of you who hate cream pie stories still have eighty or so to look forward to. Ditto for those who call me a racist; you will get another seventy or so interracial stories.

Those who hate wimps will only see about fifty more of those because the stories I sent to the I Watch category were split 50/50 between what some call wimps and some call "real men." Why the 50/50 split? It came from listening to the readers. I would get feedback asking me why all the men in my stories were hard asses. "In real life men are more forgiving, especially if it is the first indiscretion." So I would write stories with forgiving husbands and boyfriends and then the next batch of feedback would say, "Why are all your husbands spineless wimps" and I'd write stories that went back the other way.

Eventually I came to realize that I was wasting my time - there was no way I could write a story that would satisfy everybody and that is when I adopted my philosophy of writing for my own enjoyment and then offering to share.

As far as the gangbang stories? Well, what can I say? Gangbangs are gangbangs and there are still eighty or so of them to go.

The bottom line is that Literotica readers are going to see more of my old stories than my new ones. If I'm still around three or four years from now it will probably go the other way, more new than old.

I feel the need to respond to some of the comments and emails I have received. By far the largest percentage comes from people who say, "You are an asshole because all women are not whores and sluts and that's all you make them out to be."

Next most common is, "You must really hate women you sick fuck."

"You must be a wimp because all the men in your stories are wimps" is up there in the top ten along with, "Why don't you give it a rest and go crawl off in a hole somewhere."

There is a lot more, but I'm only going to address those four and in reverse order.

I won't stop and go crawl in a hole because I am enjoying the hell out of what I am doing and remember what I said, I am doing this for MY OWN ENJOYMENT and then I offer to share. Some obviously like my sharing with them and so I will continue to do so. No one is holding a gun to a reader's head and telling them they must click on a Just Plain Bob story or die. It is a conscious choice on the reader's part to move that mouse and click on that story.

When a man finds out he has a cheating wife or girlfriend there are only a limited number of ways he can handle it. If he loves her he can forgive, try to forget and try to hold on and somehow make things work. He can turn his back on her, walk away and get on with his life. The third option is to take revenge.

According to a good portion of those who send me feedback the first and second options are proof that the men are wimps. If the man takes the third option he is still considered a wimp if he doesn't do some sort of physical damage to the woman and her lover. These readers believe that the only way not to be a wimp is to kill, maim and destroy everything in sight. Doing that however, will invariably get the man throw in jail and that is why it so rarely happens in real life.

In real life most revenge takes place in the man's head when he says to himself, "I should have _____ (fill in the blank) the fucking cunt!" I know this because I have been there and done that (see The Dark Trilogy). In my stories I try to mirror real life so kill, maim and destroy are going to be for the most part absent. Outside of some fisticuffs there will be very little physical violence in my stories. Most of my husbands are going to do what I did, what several of my friends and others that I know have done, forgive, or walk away. If this makes them wimps and me a wimp for writing the story that way, so be it.

Next is the "I must hate all women." Nothing could be farther from the truth. I love women. I lust after women. I even like whores and sluts. I have been married four times, engaged two other times (that did not end in marriage) and I have always had girlfriends between marriages. My philosophy is that women were put on this earth for me to enjoy and I'm not talking just sexually. I could sit at the mall (and have) for hours and just girl watch.

The engagements, girlfriends and three of the four marriages bring me to the #1 anti JPB comment on the list.

"You are an asshole because all women aren't whores and sluts."

Well dear reader, you can not prove that by me! I will say up front that I KNOW all women aren't whores and sluts, BUT the majority of the women in my life were. My mother ran around on my father for years while he was driving a truck for a living. My Aunt Margaret cheated regularly on my Uncle Bill, as did my Aunt Mildred on my Uncle Paul. My Aunt Betty fucked around on my Uncle Bob for years and finally left him for his brother, my Uncle Wendell. Uncle Wendell in turn caught her on her knees at his company Christmas party giving Season's Greetings to his boss.

My sister is three times divorced and each divorce came about when the then current husband caught her out spreading pollen. Both of the engagements I mentioned ended when I found out that I was not the one and only and a lot of the girls I dated between marriages never made it to engagement status for the same reason.

And that brings me to my three ex-wives. The first one, Helen (I believe I commented on her in the intro to The Dark Trilogy) had seven different lovers before I found out what was going on. I was living proof that love is blind. Ditto with my second wife. She had a secret life that she hid from me and when I found out about her brother, his friends and the gangbangs she was history.

My third marriage ended in divorce because of a different kind of cheating (and I can just imagine the outrage I am going to get over this) - she cheated on me with an idea. I was away from home on business, she was lonely, a couple of Jehovah's Witnesses knocked on the door and my wife, with nothing better to do invited them in. When I came home from my trip I found out that she had found God. On a scale that runs from TRUE BELIEVER on one end to ATHEIST on the other you will find me just to the right of AGNOSTIC and since I would not allow myself to be SAVED the marriage eventually died.

So yes, I write about sluts and whores because as everyone knows, you tend to write about the things you know. And I do like sluts and whores, just not the ones that lie to me and cheat on me.

So be forewarned - if you click on a Just Plain Bob story you will be getting sluts, whores and husbands who do not kill, maim and destroy. There are other things you will rarely find in a Just Plain Bob story. Even though I try to mirror real life my stories all take place in StoryLand. In StoryLand STDs and un-wanted pregnancies do not exist unless the author feels like they may add something to the story. Bad things do not happen in StoryLand unless the author so wills it and no amount of "You should have..." in comments and feedback will change a story already posted.

Lastly, I will touch on a truth. None of what I have written here means shit because the same readers will still read the same stories that they profess to hate and make the same comments they have always made. Knowing this, I will deliberately post stories that will have them frothing at the mouth.

It is the least I can do for an adoring public.

Thank you!

Just Plain Bob
justplainbob@awesomeauthors.org